I0566019

Poetic Reflections
on Life
by
Elliot M. Rubin

...a fabulous collection
of contemporary free verse poems,
sure to hold your interest, touch
your heart, and bring a smile
to your face

cover by Marcos-Paulo-Prado at Unsplash.com

poetic
reflections
on life

by

elliot m rubin

Copyright May 2021
Library of Congress
ISBN #978-1-7363641-3-0

Dedication
To my grandchildren
Shane, Isabelle, Jonathan, Carter,
Alexandra, Melanie, Mollie, and Madison

In memory of my father
Herman S. Rubin
who wrote poetry all his life

preface
I believe poetry is to be read and understood by all. It needs to be written in plain language for everyone's enjoyment.

Too often, poets write in-depth, penetrating poems where you need to be well-read and/or versed in literature nuances to appreciate the poetry, not this book or any of my writings. I try to write so everyone can enjoy a few moments of intellectual satisfaction without consulting a dictionary or encyclopedia.

Table of Contents

bookstore

chain bookstores
have rows after rows
of neatly placed books–
rich wood-paneled walls
give an elegant aura
to browsing,
not unlike a tall,
thin, couture dressed
elegant woman
wearing strands
of mikimoto pearls

personally
i prefer small
used bookstores–
  musty,
    aged,
finding a familiar treasure on a shelf
  smells of old paper
    attracts my senses
similar to a lover
you've been with for years;
feels comfortable,
familiar,
having explored
every curve, crevice,
and emotion,
longing
to be with them forever,
never leaving their arms

tomorrow again

every day is tomorrow again
meeting new friends
tasting foods for the first time
feeling love with smiles

doesn't matter
that yesterday
is the same as today
or tomorrow is the same

dementia does not distinguish

coffee

she sits on the last stool
far down the counter
in the corner of a diner
nursing a ceramic cup
of fresh coffee with
a buttered roll
on a plate set
to the side

midnight is not so hectic;
the late movie crowd
wanders in
filling a few booths,
friends have a snack,
noise level rises

she feels morose,
the crowd ignored–
self-pity lingers in her mind,
swirling just poured milk
mesmerizes her
by the floating pattern

slowly the cup
is brought to her lips,
the moisture brings memories
of her last lover, his death,
kisses they exchanged,
lips lonely for a tender touch
with a heart crying silently,
as the coffee cup is emptied
time after time
till the sun comes up,
then she leaves

on a walk

on my walk today
i notice the mailboxes
on my street
are all the same,
a wooden post
stuck in the ground
with a black tin box
attached on top,
a door which quickly pulls down,
all indistinguishable
from each other

then i saw a different one;
it stood out from the others
red brick,
shapely,
built larger on top
with a locked door box
encased in bricks,
impervious to powerful gusts,
sturdy, well built,
nothing will affect it

that mailbox reminds me of you;
except i don't have a key
to open your heart–
i'm moving to a new house,
my mailbox will be #2

love

in school
kids laughed
when she spoke–
embarrassed
her stutter
was severe,
humiliating
until she met
The One
who cherished her,
as he stuttered
i love you

her

in the quiet times of life
she waltzes into my mind
arms draped around my neck
soft lips, tender kisses,
never leaving, always there,
reminding me of what i miss
when i made the wrong choice

virus locks

so many locks,
people can't go out,
waiting
for the golden key

no one can find it
everyone waits,
anticipates,
a key to unlock
their quarantine

the key is duplicated
yet two
are not enough
to go around

still, they wait
    locked in
while more
are made,
to arrive someday

soon...
they are told

1958

i was thirteen, she fourteen,
a full grade above me in school
yet all the kids know her,
but i am invisible

with bleached blond hair,
pink streaks running through
she was thin and beautiful,
no, gorgeous;
upon reflection
probably orgasmic looking–
i am surprised the school
didn't have her walk around
with a paper bag over her head,
she was a distraction to all the boys

one day after school dismissal
i saw her hop into a car with
four high school boys,
all giggling and laughing,
expecting a good time
based on a perceived reputation

today at seventy-five, i saw
her picture on a senior dating site–
the pink is gone along with her youth,
yet her memory is seared in my mind,
she is forever ageless

miss applegarth

the rocking chair creaks
with every slow
back and forth,
legs ache,
bulge with
purple spaghetti veins
while weathered hands
grip the wood arms
as a fluffed pillow
cushions
a hard slat seat
to comfort an old lady
while a tabby cat
stretches across her lap
purrs,
as its ears
are softly rubbed

at ninety-two
time has no meaning,
the past is spent,
the future limited,
she lives in the present

waiting

nameless

retired, looking out
my window one winter morning
at canada geese sitting
on snow-covered grass

don't know why my mind
goes back decades,
    places me on the subway
    going home from college
    one spring afternoon,
when a girl at the other end
of an almost empty train smiles at me

holding on to overhead grab rails
the train sways left to right
as it races forward
rumbling on the tracks
to the next station

i smile back at her

she looks like a movie ingenue
with freckles framed by a pixie cut
waiting for me to walk over,
to make the first move,
to say something

i'm about to be engaged
to my future wife–
my legs won't move,
my mind uncertain   what to do

when the train arrives
at the next station,   she walks off

touching flowers

i walk past the flower shop
in the market when
a display of color,
bunches tightly
wrapped in clear thin plastic
sit in pots of water,
delicate petals in every hue,
catch my eye

too many to only see one stand out,
too many to buy each one,
i walk by although
i want to grab them all
when a mother and young daughter
stops to look–
mom protesting they can't buy one,
food comes first–
the little girl reaches out
to touch a flower,
the silky softness,
a sweet aroma brings a smile
to her tiny face,
then inscribes the moment
in her memory

night time horrors

at night the dead
roam the streets,
zombies everywhere,
evil happens to those
who wander out

luckily, at 3am
i only wander
around my home
in a bathrobe,
thinking about poetry
instead of counting sheep

nassau street, manhattan

down the block
from the stock exchange
a dive bar
caters to brokers,
traders,
young office workers
who drink together
while topless women
fill glasses with ice-cold beer,
or shots of top-shelf liquor
after billions of dollars
worth of stock
changes hands
    only hours before–
twenty dollar tips
are not uncommon
for female bartenders
when they smile,
lean over
to get closer,
with music thumping
in the background,
as they smile,
then jiggle with cocktails
safely
behind the bar

thought i was special

when we kissed,
your sweet lips
                   were pure ecstasy

my heart filled
                   with love
when you whispered

                   forever

i didn't realize
what you meant

                   until you left

lust (a little ditty)

it's nice, she said,
for the company in bed;
  she thrust her bust
  in throes of lust
her cheeks bright red
while she loves him dead
  just so you know
  she's no young fertile doe

all night long
just like the song
  she's a free lovin' girl
  whose wings unfurl
just show her the sheet
she can't be beat

goodbye

as the troopship
loads the soldiers,
she stood
at the far end of the dock
watching in silence,
clutching tissues,
lips a quiver,
tears moist on the lids,
eyes searching
the edge of the grey deck
at the men, née boys,
lined up waving
as she looks for her fiancé

the ship's horn blows one long blast,
thick heavy ropes
untie from the dock,
tug boats readied in place
the ship starts to pull away
sailing out to sea

she raises her hand to wave,
silently offering a prayer
for his safe return,
while rubbing a small
engagement broach
softly between her fingers,
finally allowing a tear to flow

jersey city wedding

it was an irish polish wedding–
the hall was in the rear of a bar,
every table had a pitcher of beer while
a waiter takes the straight shot orders

young basha is polish; she taught me
to polka as we hopped around
together while a three-piece band
played, until my mother-in-law's
friend, "big ann" cut in

she was taller than me, heavyset,
and literally picked me up,
held me close
as she bounced around the floor
with my face buried deep in her bosom,
only coming up for air when
her feet landed on the ground

the party's over, groom's father, way over
six feet tall and four hundred pounds
is soused. friends carried him out, put him
on the hood of his car, then drove him
around the block to his home while they
reach out the windows
holding a leg and an arm
so he didn't fall off

nothing

after years together
he strayed,
then left
after his mistress
is with child,
leaving a wife
with crushed dreams,
an unfulfilled womb,
and a pillow filled with tears

threads

my old, worn-out sweater,
loose strings hanging
ready to be clipped

removing them one by one,
each reminds me
of the times
it kept me warm

i wore it
    when:
        i asked her to be my wife–
        we brought our children home
            after their birth–
        at my kid's school graduation–

        the ambulance took her away

the cut threads are put in a drawer
safely kept with my dreams of the past–
every night when i turn over in bed
remembering her face
    missing her

my life now
is a cut thread,
missing
from the rest of the garment

normal

after she asked me to check it
your temperature is normal
then thought to myself,
what is normal?

small talk with friends at night
in a bistro or bar, breakfast with
a lover after a night exhausted,
or to get dressed, then go to work?

is it normal when she puckers for a kiss,
gently places her arms around my neck,
wraps her legs around me tight
says i love you every night
because i'm the only person in her sight?

normal is not normal during a pandemic,
it changes to a new constant normal;
one we get used to, cause there is no other–
i want my old normal back, normally

baseball treasure

growing up in brooklyn
the hometown team was the
dodgers, always
the perennial runnerup

wait till next year
was the team's motto,
always a bridesmaid
never a bride, not
winning a world series,
coming close, never won

till 1955-
when they finally won
their first world series–
car horns honk
on flatbush avenue,
people scream out
apartment windows,
ecstasy ruled in brooklyn

today, tucked away
in a wells fargo bank vault
secured by an armed guard,
is an original
1955 brooklyn dodgers team photo
encased in an archival
plastic sleeve

a doctor visit

when i was first married
i moved to the small town
where my wife grew up,
then used her old world war two
battlefield hardened
family doctor and nurse

she needed a check-up
for school; i went with her–
his practice was in his home
with two adjoining exam rooms

the door between the rooms
was slightly ajar as i sat on a low stool,
my wife sitting on the exam table as
we waited for the doctor

his old, no-nonsense nurse came in–
for some unknown reason, she started to
lecture me that once you get syphilis,
you have it forever

sitting on the stool, i notice a senior
couple in the next exam room
bend forward, peering into our room,
strangely looking at me!

naani poetry

bye

there she goes
i'm not at her side anymore
she told me she loves me
i didn't answer back

naani poetry consists of 4 lines,
total lines consist of 20-25 syllables
can be any subject

no color

two people
no clothes
bodies meld
limbs tangled
feel the heat
feel the passion
fluids commingle

there is no skin color
  nor should there be
    love is blind
too bad society is not

books

he is in every chapter
in her autobiography
from page one through
to the end, where
they date, move in,
live together–
he leaves her
in the next to last chapter
for a pert, younger girl–
in the final one
she wins the lottery,
moves to a mansion,
has a boy toy,
then starts a new
chapter in her life
waving goodbye
to her old lover–
then ends the book

time to stop

hair is long
life is short
lived a full one
done this and that
able to survive

finger joints ache,
the guitar put away
no more music,
shows canceled,
no more crowds
the curtain finally down

yet the music
still plays,
needs to be heard,
it roams in my mind
never ending

8th street station, NYC

doesn't matter if it's night
                            or day
the subway never stops–
  it's the lifeblood of manhattan,
carries people to work
or lovers on a date,
the parade of people
continues to
    walk-on
     walk-off
always movement

from the black entrails
of the rat-infested tunnel
clickety-clack echos
off the dark, soot-stained walls
                            as the train

THRUSTS itself into the station
pushing hot, stagnant air in summer,
frigid air in winter,
as it rushes by black, iron i-beams
spaced apart on the concrete station, with
a once-white metal sign, printed with a black 8–
set back against a dirt-encrusted
mosaic tile wall
is a sturdy wood bench,
bolted to the floor
as its curved seat
cradles an elderly woman
who sits there
    l o n g hours,
             odd hours, watching

until police chase her away

happiness

don't hold back
happiness,
too many people
are sad,
give a call
unexpectedly,
or a hug
or a kiss
to a loved one–
the engagement ring
in your pocket
can bring two lifetimes
of memories

a backcountry joint

with weather-beaten clapboard,
located on a rural alabama road,
is the local hot spot for booze,
blues, gambling, and girls

three short rotted wood steps
leads to a sagging front porch
where a secret knock lets you in-
although police hang there too

three grizzled grey-bearded bluesmen
play in a corner, girls dance on linoleum floors
while momma jane cooks okra, grits, and BBQ brisket
in the rear kitchen and yard
while two raggedy dogs eat the droppings

upstairs in one of the two bedrooms
a low stakes card game plays out while
pretty june campbell, with her two pigtails,
entertains men looking for love by the hour

valentines day love 2021

what is love?
   who defines it?
who authorized them to decide?

why is
   same-sex love
   inter-racial love
   trans love
not valid?

someone has to tell the proverbial **them**
   there is no such thing as bad love

forgotten

there are so many poems
i did not write–
my mind
my thoughts
   flow so fast
through my consciousness

i can't write
quick enough

overcome

fear means nothing
anymore–
self-doubt
is in the past,
i can soar
as high as i want,
fly with eagles,
run with tigers,
finish the run
win the race,
this is my time,
    finally;
i won't hold myself back anymore

strawberry summer

i watch her
pick a fresh
strawberry
from baskets
filled with them

rinses one,
holds it in her hand,
sprinkles sugar
all over,
presses it
between pink lips,
placed softly
on her tongue,
then tasting
the sweetness,
causing her face
to smile–
i wish
summer
never ends

after five decades

i looked forward
to the nights
we danced
neck to neck
in the kitchen
after dinner,
holding you
as tight as i did
on our first date
many years ago–
now i have trouble
standing, hands shake,
balance is off,
it's nice to be in bed
under the wool comforter
on a cold night,
with memories of you
to warm my heart

single malt whiskey

there's a hole
    in the bottle–
someone
has to do something
or the twelve-year-old
amber spirits will spill out

there are two
empty glasses here,
sitting on the table
next to the corkscrew

since she brought the bottle
i thought it only fair
to share it with her
as we sit
talking,
after a night out
on the town

waiting for our intoxicated
spirits to spill out too

if only

if only i started
  earlier in life–
  writing lifts my soul,
  elevates my inner being

words
i left unwritten
the world will never read,
my heart is filled
        with so many

i race
  at four in the morning
  to put them down on paper
  before they evaporate at dawn

if only i started
  earlier in life

chickita

she was a rock 'n' roll girl,
heavy metal, acid rock
it didn't matter;
tall, lanky, with wooden
beaded earrings hanging down,
a blouse half open, no bra
while the bands played
in dingy dive bars
she drank double boilermakers,
    top shelf only–
wherever this one guitarist played,
she was there–
some said her boss is a big-time agent
who sends her to find new talent to sign–
she liked this guy a lot,
told him his name is tattooed
on her inner thigh in blue ink,
that he'd see it if they were ever together–
she offered him two contracts,
one for music, one for marriage–
    he put away his guitar, left the band
        didn't want to get married
           disappeared
years later, she made the news;
found dead from drugs
in a malibu home, on the water,
while married to a famous musician

when up in my attic,
i think of her when i look
at the dust-covered guitar case

manhattan blues in b flat

midtown, off-broadway,
a basement blues lounge
swings at dusk
when black musicians take the stage–
piano keys tinkle in treble
with bass keys running a contra tune
while a cigarette dangles
from his lips, gray ash falls
on yellowed ivory keys–
in the corner, a snare drum softly bristles
with the large drum keeping beat
while a tenor sax waits a few bars
then s l o w l y comes in, with
a hes-i-tant   wail, then

    increasing in volume—
a bass player fingers a boogie beat
to start the customer's feet tapping–
from the shadows, she walks to center stage,
a singular spotlight shines on a honey-skinned girl
with slicked black hair, a red bird tattoo on her shoulder
wearing a low cut, sparkling fitted blue dress–
she starts to sing, a little soft scat first,
then breaks out in a *blues classic*–
free salted popcorn keeps the beer flowing
while marijuana smoke fills the room,
                                        ceiling
                              the
                  to

obscures the stage, **rises**
as everyone chills out

noisy visit

after the thunderstorm
i visit my friend
who is depressed over
his recent divorce

the pot on the stove
percolates–
i hear   pop,   pop,   pop
as the brown liquid
rose to the glass cover
heating the coffee,
so we could sit,
drink, then talk a bit

while i spoke
water on the roof
drops down
on the window air conditioner
    drip,   drip,   drip,
a constant sound
contrasting with the percolator

after coffee
i pour in
whole cream,
stir the spoon,
    clink,   clink,   clink
as metal hits
the sides of the ceramic cup

we sit in silence
sipping coffee,
                with nothing to say

sox

poets
are creative people
who exhibit
certain traits–
they either
are linear thinkers
who follow
strict rules of format,
or nonconformists
who write
free verse poetry–
i fall
into the latter;
a telltale sign is
i don't match
my patterned sox,
or spell it correctly

time

in the future
a young child
sits at a screen
reading poetry
written hundreds
of years before;
mesmerized
at the humanity
in the words
of long-dead poets

today
i expect no recognition,
awards, or financial gain
from my writing,
i'm secure
in the belief
sometime in the future
my poetry will be read

time is on my side
as long as i write
quality poems,
do enough of them
to be discovered,
before
the earth is pulled into the sun

with luck,
humanity will survive
on another planet,
along with archives
of our humankind

over

yes, i know
our relationship
is over and done-
you strung me along
like a puppy on a leash

my broken heart
yearns for love again–
you walked out at
the altar of love,
yet i forgive you

you left me
a gift,
the ability
to write
a love poem

about your betrayal

a question or two

i want to ask
religious people
some questions

do you believe
a god made us
in its image?

is what that god
makes good?

if god makes
good things,
then why not
full equality
for everyone,
everywhere?

LGBTQ equality
is a right
of humanity

a beautiful rose

decades ago
i planted a rose bush;
watered,
nurtured,
protected it
until young buds appear

they bloom,
the strength
of strong stems
supports them

the prettiest rose
stands out,
admired by both
men and women,
being sought by both

the single flower
sways
back and forth
with the wind;
i wait to see
who cuts the stem
to make it theirs

cup of coffee

a small cup of coffee
is an amazing thing
for what it can accomplish

meeting a first date
  saying goodbye to a lover
a third informal job interview
  asking for a raise at lunch
friends talk after a meal

the cocoa bean picker
has no idea
what the end result
of his labors
will be

how happy or sad
it will make someone
after its crushed,
mixed with hot water,
then poured in a cup
so many miles away

midnight

the witching hour
is almost here–
in the distance
a freight train whistles
as it crosses deserted
backcountry roads,
warning
no one in particular
of its fast approach

the train rumbles
whistles fade
into the night
carrying
in my imagination
cargo packed tightly
going to a warehouse
in the middle of nowhere

homeless vagrants
in the empty freight cars
touring american vistas,
while i watch
the late news
at home
with my dog at my feet
sitting on my recliner

language of love

you are someone
special to me;
your sweetness,
unbridled kindness,
a bright smile
like the morning sun
chases away grey clouds

a lyrical love poem
in the language of love
is the minimum
you deserve

unfortunately,
being from new york
i don't know french;
but am fluent in
brooklynese

darling
please 'member
dees sincere woids
i love yous,
from my heart
to yours

true love

there's an empty spot
at the dinner table
waiting for you

it's been years
since you're gone—
i'm alone
when the sun sets
each night,
but my love for you
never sets—
the pain's still there,
your clothes
are in the bedroom closet;
i couldn't bear
to clean out
your memory
from my life

lydia 1963

on a sunny spring day
after high school let out
she asked if i wanted lunch
at wolfie's near the junction

lydia is a hippie chick,
tall, thin, waist-length
straight blonde hair
flowing down her madras blouse,
with long dangling earrings–
as we walk
she took out cigarettes
and offers one to me

it was my first smoke,
not my last;
it took me
on a sixteen-year
tobacco journey–
with every smoke
i inhaled,
i exhaled
the memory of her;
only the nodules on my lungs
are what's left of that afternoon

mental slavery

we are
all slaves
in one way or another–
we are
owned by our
mental inabilities
to break free

think about the things
we want to do,
yet don't–
the love sought;
  yet we don't see it is available,
held back sometimes
by nothing tangible,
only by ourselves

slumber

window shades are down
the morning sun is blocked
darkness lulls me to sleep–
the lawnmower outside roars

i pull the blanket over my head
seek the sleep i lost to noise
exciting dreams try to come back–
the lawnmower roars outside

twisting and turning in a warmed bed
i start to fly off in a pleasant slumber,
dreams fade away as i begin to drift off–
outside, the lawnmower roars

finally unable to sleep, wide awake,
i get out of bed, walk to my chair,
grab a book to pass the time–
the lawnmower's gone
                    quiet as the dead

Please check the author's website for more poetry books.

www.CreativeFiction.net

Instagram, his account, always has daily poems.

elliot_m_rubin

www.ingramcontent.com/pod-product-compliance
Lightning Source LLC
Chambersburg PA
CBHW071145250626
47159CB00006B/2302